Koala Challah

LAURA GEHL

ILLUSTRATIONS BY MARIA MOLA

*For the Garber/Snyder family, the
Schuchman family, and the Taylor family—
with thanks for our many wonderful Shabbat
dinners together. – L.G.*

*For those who persist and specially for my
little (angel) koala. – M.M.*

KAR-BEN PUBLISHING
A division of Lerner Publishing Group, Inc.
241 First Avenue North
Minneapolis, MN 55401 USA
1-800-4-KARBEN

Website address: www.karben.com

Main body text set in Belwe Mono Std Regular 17/25.
Typeface provided by International Typeface Corporation.

Library of Congress Cataloging-in-Publication Data

Names: Gehl, Laura, author. | Mola, Maria, illustrator.
Title: Koala challah / by Laura Gehl ; illustrated by Maria Mola.
Description: Minneapolis : Kar-Ben Publishing. [2017] | Summary: "Lila the
    koala just wants to help her family get ready for Shabbat, but she always
    ends up making a mess instead. So she spends a whole week practicing
    making challah, and comes up with the perfect recipe just in time for
    Shabbat."—Provided by publisher.
Identifiers: LCCN 2016028354| ISBN 9781512420876 (lb : alk. paper) | ISBN
    9781512420883 (pb : alk. paper)
Subjects: | CYAC: Koala—Fiction. | Challah (Bread)—Fiction. | Bread—
    Fiction. | Sabbath—Fiction. | Judaism—Customs and practices—Fiction. |
    Baking—Fiction.
Classification: LCC PZ7.G2588 Ko 2017 | DDC [E]—dc23

LC record available at https://lccn.loc.gov/2016028354

Manufactured in the United States of America
1-41257-23232-12/6/2016

Koala Challah

Lila

KAR-BEN
PUBLISHING

Every Friday afternoon, Lila watched her big sister Rachel make the eucalyptus oil candles for Shabbat dinner. Koala bears love eucalyptus!

One Friday, Lila decided to try making candles too.

"Oh, Lila, the table is a mess!" said Mommy when she came home.

"I'm sorry, Mommy," said Lila. "I just wanted to help get ready for Shabbat."

"I know you did, honey. Come, help me clean up," said Mommy.

Every Friday afternoon, Lila watched her big sister Naomi make the eucalyptus wine for Shabbat dinner. Koala bears love eucalyptus!

One Friday, Lila decided to try making wine too.

When Daddy walked in, he sighed. "Oh, Lila, the table is a mess! Please help me clean it up."

"OK, Daddy," said Lila. "I just wanted to help get ready for Shabbat."

The next Friday, Lila made a sign that said "Shabbat Shalom" and picked flowers to decorate the Shabbat table.

"Oh Lila," said Daddy. "What a mess!"

"I just wanted to help get ready for Shabbat," Lila explained.

Mommy put her arm around Lila. "I know you are trying to help, but every week we hurry to get ready for Shabbat, and every week you make a mess. Cleaning up takes so long that I hardly have time to make challah!"

"Can I make the challah next week?" asked Lila.

"Please?"

"All right," said Mommy. "But you should practice first."

So on Sunday, Lila tried to make challah.

"I think maybe I left the challah in the oven too long," Lila said.

On Monday, Lila tried again.

"Oops. I think you forgot to add the yeast," said Rachel." That's why the challah didn't rise."

On Tuesday, Lila made sure to use yeast.

"Uh-oh," said Naomi. "I think you put in too much salt."

On Wednesday, the challah crumbled when
Lila tried to put it on a plate.

On Thursday, Lila's challah looked beautiful. "I brushed egg on the dough before I baked it," Lila explained proudly. "That's why the bread is so shiny."

"It tastes fine," Naomi said, eating the first piece.

"Yes, fine," Rachel agreed.

Lila tasted the challah. Her sisters were right. It was . . .
fine. But Lila wanted her challah to be better than fine.

That night Lila lay awake in bed. She wanted her challah to be as special as Rachel's beautiful eucalyptus oil candles and Naomi's delicious eucalyptus oil wine. She wanted it to be wonderful!

On Friday afternoon, Lila made two loaves of challah. This time, she added a special ingredient. She wanted it to be the yummiest challah ever!

At Shabbat dinner, Rachel lit the candles she had made. Naomi poured the wine she had made. And Lila uncovered her challah loaves.

"This is the yummiest challah I have ever eaten!" Mommy exclaimed.

Lila smiled. "I call it KOALA CHALLAH. It has a special ingredient, our favorite food — eucalyptus!"

"It looks like you found the perfect way to help get ready for Shabbat," Daddy said. "We all love eucalyptus, but what's *most* special, Lila, is that you didn't give up and you made the challah in your own special way."

. . . And after dinner they all cleaned up the kitchen together.